DATE DUE		

PRAIRIE SCHOOL
1530 BRANDYWYN LANE
BUFFALO GROVE, IL 60089

THE SECRETS OF DROON

Journey
to the
Volcano Palace

by Tony Abbott

Illustrated by David Merrell

Cover illustration by Tim Jessell

A
LITTLE APPLE
PAPERBACK

SCHOLASTIC INC.
New York Toronto London Auckland Sydney
Mexico City New Delhi Hong Kong

Book design by Dawn Adelman

ISBN 0-590-10841-7

Text copyright © 1999 by Robert T. Abbott.
Illustrations copyright © 1999 by Scholastic Inc.
All rights reserved. Published by Scholastic Inc.
SCHOLASTIC, APPLE PAPERBACKS, and associated logos
are trademarks and/or registered trademarks of Scholastic Inc.

24

5 6 7 8 9/0

Printed in the U.S.A.
First Scholastic printing, June 1999

40

To Mrs. Schwarz
and her wonderful class of
wizards in training

Contents

One

Dreams

Eric Hinkle couldn't breathe.

The air around him was dark and smoky and hot. The evil sorcerer Lord Sparr was after him, chasing him down a long, dark tunnel.

"Now that you know my secret," Sparr shouted, "you will never be able to leave!"

"I don't know any secret!" Eric pleaded. "Let me go! Let me out of Droon!"

"NEVER!" was Sparr's only word.

The sorcerer's eyes were filled with anger. The weird fins behind his ears were purple and shiny. He was getting closer. Closer!

The tunnel ahead of Eric split in two.

Go right! said a voice in his head.

"Oh, man!" Eric swallowed hard. He had always had a problem with right and left. He looked at his hands. Which was right? It took him a second to decide. "This way!" he said.

He charged ahead into one of the tunnels.

No! said the voice in his head. *The right one!*

"Ha! Now I have you!" Sparr shrieked as Eric ran up against a solid wall. "My secret is safe!"

"Help!" Eric cried. "I'm trapped!"

Sparr lunged.

Eric leaped out of the way.

Thud!

"Ouch!" Eric groaned.

He opened his eyes. He was in his room. He was half on the floor, half still in bed, wound up tight in his bedsheet. He looked like a mummy.

"Whoa!" he said. "What a nightmare."

The door opened. His mother stood in the doorway. "Eric, what was that noise?"

"Uh, I guess I fell out of bed," Eric said, unwinding himself from his sheet. "But I'm okay."

Mrs. Hinkle helped him up. "By the way, Eric. Where is Droon?"

Eric nearly fell to the floor again. "Huh?"

"You were talking in your sleep," his mother said. "Something about a place called Droon."

Eric gulped. He blinked. His mouth opened to answer, but nothing came out.

Droon was a secret. No one was supposed to know about the incredible world he and his friends had found under his basement stairs.

Galen the wizard had made them promise not to tell anyone.

The problem was, ever since his first time in Droon, Eric couldn't think of anything else.

Now he was even *dreaming* about it.

And Princess Keeah had told them that when you dreamed about Droon, it meant you would go back.

"Uh, Droon is a place we, uh . . . made up," Eric said. "Neal and Julie and I."

He hated to lie. But until he and his friends found out more about Droon — and about the evil Sparr — it wasn't safe for people to know.

"Sounds secret," his mother said. "By the way, your friends called. They're coming over."

Eric dressed quickly. He had to tell Neal and Julie about his dream right away.

He got to the backyard in time to see a small, scruffy dog chasing Neal across the lawn.

Grrr! The dog kept biting Neal's feet.

"Stop it, Snorky!" Neal tossed a biscuit across the yard. The dog bounced after it. "Hey, Eric."

"I'm glad you're here," Eric said. "It happened. I had a weird dream about Droon —"

"Not me." Neal shook his head. "I was so tired teaching Snorky to fetch, I fell asleep before I hit the pillow. Actually, I fell asleep on my floor."

"I woke up on the floor!" Eric said. "It

was weird. It felt like someone from Droon was *sending* the dream to me."

At that moment, Julie came into the yard.

Eric ran over to her. "Julie, something strange is going on —"

"First, let me tell you about my dream," Julie said. "I was in Droon —"

"Me, too!" Eric gasped. "Sparr was chasing me because I knew his big secret. But I forget what the secret was."

"Hmm." Julie bit her lip. She always did that when she was trying to figure something out. "I was at a pool of water. I was really thirsty and I wanted to take a drink, but something creeped me out. I forget what it was, but it was very yucky."

Grrr! Snorky ran back across the lawn. He fastened his teeth on the toe of Neal's right sneaker.

"Let go of my shoe!" Neal cried. "Wait a

second. . . . I remember now. I had a scary dream, too! I forget most of it, except . . ."

"Except for what?" Julie asked.

Neal shrugged. "I remember it was about my feet. I was in Droon, and my feet hurt."

Snorky leaped suddenly for Neal's left shoe.

"Heel!" Neal snapped, shaking his foot.

"Well, he's *eating* your heel," Julie said.

"Maybe he's learning!" Neal tossed another biscuit, and Snorky ran for it. "Let's get inside."

The three kids jumped up the back steps into Eric's kitchen and headed for the basement.

"Droon is full of secrets," said Julie. "Secrets we need answers to. We need to go back."

Neal frowned. "But what if all of our dreams come true? I mean, my dream was pretty weird."

"There's only one way to find out," said Eric.

They tramped down the stairs into the basement. It was messy. It was beyond messy. Eric knew he'd have to clean it one of these days.

Cleaning all the old toys and junk out of the basement was his special project. Neal and Julie had said they would help.

When we get back, Eric thought.

He pulled open the little door under the stairs. They entered a small, empty room.

They closed the door. They all held their breath as Eric switched off the light.

Whoosh! The floor vanished beneath them.

In its place was a long flight of stairs. The steps shimmered in the light from below.

The light from the land of Droon.

"Yes! We *are* going back," Eric whispered. "I wonder where the stairs will lead us this time."

"Or if it's day or night in Droon," said Neal.

"Let's stop talking and find out," said Julie.

The three friends stepped slowly down the stairs. The air was hushed and cool. And the sky below them turned deep blue and sparkled like a million jewels.

A giant moon cast golden light on the stairs.

"Nighttime," Eric whispered.

Before they knew it, the three friends were in Droon once again.

Two

Sands of Time

A wide sea of sand stretched away as far as the eye could see. Sand hills — dunes — rolled and dipped all the way to the horizon.

"Wow!" Neal said. "This is my first desert."

The moonbeams made the dunes glitter with golden light.

"This is awesome," Julie said. "Droon is beautiful at night."

Eric breathed in the cool air. "Let's climb over that dune," he said, pointing to one of the high, curving hills of sand. "For a look."

They stepped down from the bottom step.

The sand was warm.

They climbed to the top of the dune and peered over.

Not far away was a striped tent. Shaggy, six-legged beasts stood outside. The kids remembered them from their first time in Droon. The beasts were called pilkas.

"Somebody's camping," Neal whispered.

Eric noticed a strange purple flag flying over the tent. "Careful," he said. "You never know what you might find."

"We don't have much choice," said Julie, pointing behind them. "The stairs are fading."

The three friends watched as the rainbow-colored steps vanished in the sky.

"I hope we find them again later," Neal said. "Wherever they are."

Slowly, they approached the tent. A large flap hung down over an opening.

"Let's peek in," Julie whispered.

Suddenly, a voice spoke from inside the tent. "Come in!"

Julie held her breath and pulled up the flap.

The three friends looked inside.

Their friend Princess Keeah was sitting on a rug spread out over the sand. She was dressed in a light blue tunic. In her long blonde hair she wore a golden crown.

Next to her sat the old wizard, Galen Longbeard, and his assistant, Max.

Lining the inside of the tent were piles of extra-plump purple-colored pillows.

"Welcome back!" Keeah said, laughing when she saw the kids.

"We've all been waiting for you!" Max

chirped happily. Max was a spider troll. He had eight legs and could spin sticky webs and climb up walls. But his face was pudgy like a troll's, and his bright orange hair sprouted straight up.

Eric smiled as he and his friends entered the tent. "How did you know we were coming?"

"I can see the future!" Keeah said.

Julie gasped. "You can?"

"Keeah," said Galen sternly, "you must respect your real magic powers. You should not invent others you don't have . . . yet."

The princess made a face. "I'm sorry." She turned to the three friends. "Actually, I can't see the future. I just dreamed about all of you, and I guessed you were on your way."

Eric shot looks at Julie and Neal. "We had dreams, too. But we didn't understand them."

"In Droon, wizards — and sorcerers — can use dreams as messengers," Galen said. "Sometimes they foretell what will happen. We may understand more at dawn, when we begin —"

Neal tugged a purple pillow over to the rug.

"Hey!" the pillow snarled. "You pinched me! I was having the nicest nap, too!"

Neal jumped up. "Whoa . . . sorry!" He looked around. "Wait, did that pillow just talk to me?"

Max chirped in laughter. "That's a Lumpy!"

Neal made a face. "Lumpy or not, in the Upper World, pillows don't talk!"

Keeah smiled. "Max means it's not a pillow you sat on. It's a Lumpy. A purple Lumpy!"

It was then that the kids noticed small round faces on the chubby pillows. Their cheeks bulged, and their noses were like purple tennis balls.

One of the creatures stood up, stretched, and yawned. It had short, fat arms and squat legs.

"I am Khan," he said. "King of the purple Lumpies of Lumpland. Just over the last dune on your left. We Lumpies are the best desert trackers in Droon. We sniff out trouble." He paused to sniff the air. "Danger is everywhere!"

"Uh . . . pleased to meet you!" Eric said.

Galen rose, wrapping his long blue robe around him. "Now, come outside. We must talk about tomorrow."

The air outside the tent was cool and sweet.

"It sure is peaceful here," Julie said.

"It wasn't yesterday," Keeah told them. "That's the reason we're here."

"What happened?" Eric asked.

"Lord Sparr," Khan said, shaking his purple fist in the air. "He nearly destroyed one of our villages with his red jewel. Luckily, the terrible flame burned his hand, and he fled."

Eric remembered the red jewel. It was called the Red Eye of Dawn. The sorcerer Sparr had stolen it from Keeah and was planning to use it to take over Droon.

"The Eye of Dawn commands the forces of nature," Galen said. "Fire, wind, wave, and sky. It is *very* powerful. Yesterday, Droon was lucky. Tomorrow, we may not be."

Keeah pointed across the desert. "We think Sparr fled to his secret palace. It's in a hidden land called Kano."

Galen turned grim. "A terrible place, dangerous and deadly. Sparr will not expect us to go."

Neal nodded. "We'd be dumb to do that."

"And because he doesn't expect it," Keeah added, "that's exactly what we'll do!"

The three kids were silent.

Eric blinked. "Dangerous and deadly?"

Khan nodded. "And the Lumpies shall lead you right to it!"

"We must find the Eye before Sparr uses it again," Galen said. "Droon itself is at stake."

"Are you in?" Keeah asked.

Eric looked at Julie, then at Neal. He knew they were just as afraid as he was.

"I guess we're in," Julie said.

"Get the maps," Neal said. "I'd like to see exactly where we're going."

Max chuckled. "Maps will be of no help! Lord Sparr lives in a volcano!"

Three

The Oasis at Noon

Moments later, the sun began to rise over the distant dunes.

"It's time!" Keeah said.

They all climbed to the rim of a tall, curving sand dune. Galen pointed to the sandy plains where the sun was rising.

"The door to Kano lies in the East," the wizard said. "According to a legend, it can be seen where it is not."

Eric nodded slowly. "Okay. Got it. Great. Um . . . could you say that again?"

"It's a riddle," Max said, scurrying back and forth in the sand. "No one knows exactly where Sparr's palace is."

Julie began biting her lip again. "Then how are we going to find the door to Kano?"

But Galen was already walking back down the dune. "By finding the answer to the riddle!"

"First things first," Khan said. "Our journey of many miles begins with a single sniff!" He sniffed the air, then pointed. "East is that way!"

Within moments, Khan and his Lumpies packed up the tent and supplies.

"Into the East!" Max chirped.

Hrrr! Galen's shaggy pilka, Leep, whinnied in excitement as the kids piled onto her back.

"We're off!" cried Julie.

They rode for hours over the hot dunes.

Mile after mile, they saw nothing but burning white sand.

"I think we're lost," Neal said, wiping his forehead. "I mean, I guess we're in the East, but I don't see any doors. All I see are two things. Sand, and more sand."

Eric pointed into the distance. "What's that?"

It looked like a shadow against the far-away dunes, a grove of trees waving in the breeze.

"Is it a mirage?" Julie said. "You know, the imaginary things you see in the desert that aren't really there?"

"Imaginary," Eric sighed. "Right now I'm imagining the town pool filled with cool water."

"You want water, you got it," Neal said.

"I'm gonna be a puddle in about three minutes."

"No, you won't," Keeah said. "That's an oasis! We can rest there and get some real water!"

They rode quickly and soon reached a group of tall palm trees sprouting up from the dunes.

In the center was a pool of cool, blue water.

Eric and his friends slid down from Leep and moved into the shade of the waving palm trees.

"This isn't the pool in my dream," Julie said. "There's nothing yucky about this."

"Good!" Neal exclaimed. "Because I'm *way* past thirsty." He and Julie and Keeah went to the near side of the pool and began to drink.

The Lumpies led the pilkas over. They all bent their heads to the water.

"Drink up," Khan said. "It may be many miles before we find water again."

Eric scrambled to an open spot on the side of the pool. He breathed in the sweet air under the trees, then bent down, cupping his hands together. The shimmering water looked so refreshing.

He stooped to take a big sip.

He froze solid at what he saw.

"What is it?" Keeah said, looking up.

Eric stared into the pool. "My reflection —"

Neal laughed. "Yeah, you look pretty grimy!"

"We all do," Julie added.

"No, that's not it," Eric mumbled. In the surface of the pool he saw his face. Behind his head were the tops of the palm trees that he knew were waving in the wind behind him.

And behind the palm trees . . . was an

enormous gate! A gate made of black iron, towering up behind the palms.

Eric whirled around and looked up.

There was no gate behind the palm trees.

He turned back to the pool. The gate was there, in the reflection, standing as huge and as plain as day!

"An invisible gate!" he gasped. "Like the riddle says — it can be seen where it is not!"

"What?" Neal said, slurping from his hands.

"We're here!" Eric cried. "I see it in the pool. The door to Kano. But it's *not* in the pool. It's *there*!" He pointed up behind him, beyond the palm trees. "The entrance to Kano is right there!"

Galen rushed over. Max scurried across the sand. Keeah, Neal, and Julie ran to Eric.

They all stared at the open air behind the palms, then at the pool.

"It's there, all right," Keeah said. "But it's still invisible. How do we get in?"

"I have an idea." Neal stooped to the pool and filled his hands with water. He hurried through the palm trees to where the gates would be.

He tossed the water across the air.

Sssss! The water struck something in midair and spilled down it.

Suddenly, there it was! A patch of black iron!

Julie tried it next.

Sssss! More of the black gate appeared.

Everyone joined in, even the Lumpies. They cupped their hands. They used buckets. They even filled their boots with water.

Splish! Splosh! Splursh!

Soon, the entire gate dripped into shape

before them. It stood huge and glistening behind the tall palm trees of the oasis.

Galen stood back in awe. "Behold! We have discovered the way to Sparr's secret realm! This is the door to Kano!"

Four

Into Sparr's Realm

The iron gate towered high above the dunes, casting its dark shadow over the oasis.

"Quickly! Quickly!" Khan shouted to the pilkas. The shaggy creatures nudged the black gate. Again and again they pushed against it.

Max sat on Leep's head, urging her on. "Hurry, the water is drying! The gate will disappear!"

Errr, errr! The giant door began to creak open.

"Yes!" Eric gulped. "We've done it."

Everyone slipped through.

Klang! The gate closed loudly behind them.

Right away, the air was hotter. It was hazy and brown and bad-smelling. Not clear and pinkish-blue like over the rest of Droon.

"We've entered Sparr's hidden empire," Max chirped. "This is the nasty land of Kano!"

"Stinky," Khan mumbled to his fellow Lumpies. "As I expected."

Galen nodded to himself and smiled as he looked around at the smoky brown air. "Yes, this is good. Very good!"

Neal coughed. "Excuse me, sir, but what's so good? This place is so smelly I can hardly breathe!"

"There are no Ninns at the gate," the

wizard replied. "That means that Lord Sparr does not yet know we are here. But we must hurry."

They climbed back on the pilkas and rode ahead. Before long the small band found itself standing on a steep ridge. A sudden wind swept across them. The dark air cleared for a second.

They stood above a deep, black valley.

The ground was dark and burnt for miles. It was easy to see the reason why. In the middle of the valley was a giant black cone.

It looked like a tall mountain, except that its top was torn open. And a huge pool of lava splashed and spurted and bubbled in the middle.

"A volcano!" Julie gasped.

"That is the heart of Kano, the black mountain home of Lord Sparr," Galen told them. "Come."

The wizard galloped into the lead. Max clung to his pilka's mane, while Leep, with the children on her back, trotted alongside. Khan and his purple Lumpies rode close behind them all.

They made their way quietly but quickly to the center of the valley.

"Maybe Sparr's not home," Neal whispered. "That would be pretty good."

"I hope Sparr *is* here," Keeah said as they rode closer. "I want to fight him as he fought my mother. Besides, wherever he is, the Eye is, too."

Neal, Eric, and Julie knew Keeah blamed Sparr for the disappearance of her mother, Queen Relna. Two years before, the queen had fought Sparr in a fierce battle. She was never seen again.

Galen spurred his pilka quickly to the mountain. "Khan and I will scout for the entrance to the volcano palace. In the meantime — beware of fire monsters!"

Neal blinked and looked at Julie. "Did he say *fire* monsters?"

Eric clambered up onto a long, crusted rock that lay in front of the mountain. "Maybe the entrance is behind these big stones."

"What do you see?" Keeah called out.

"Not much," Eric said. "Wait, there *is* an opening! We can go in — hey! This rock just moved!"

"Uh, I don't think it's a rock," Julie said, pointing to a big green eyeball flicking open just under Eric's foot. I think it's . . . it's . . . a monster!"

Hrooosh! A column of fire spurted from the beast's mouth, burning the black ground blacker.

"A fire monster!" Neal shouted.

Suddenly, another stony-gray shape shook itself. A large green eye opened on it, too. It thrust its head up into the air. *Hrooosh!*

"Two fire monsters!" Neal shouted.

Galen charged over. "Get inside!" he yelled to the children. Then he leaped onto the back of one monster and began wrestling with it.

"Lumpies, help the wizard!" Khan called out. Instantly his Lumpies jumped on the second monster. They pinched it and poked it with all their might.

"Max, Khan, lead the children through!" Galen shouted.

The stone-skinned monsters thrashed and twisted, but Galen and the Lumpies kept on fighting.

"We can't leave you!" Keeah cried.

"You must!" the wizard commanded. "Find the Eye! It is the only way to save —"

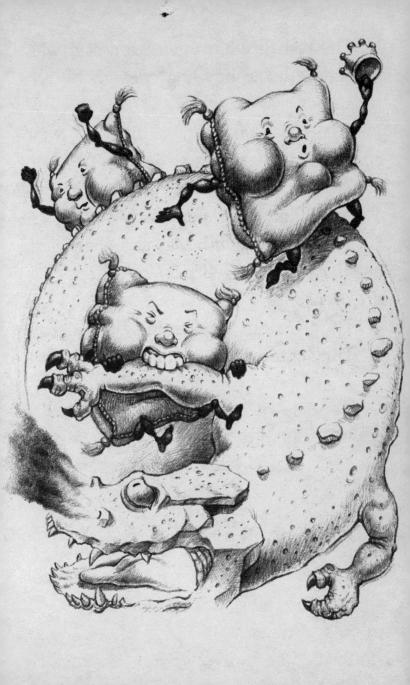

The rest of what the wizard said was lost beneath the howling cries of the fire beasts.

"Galen can take care of himself," Max chittered.

Khan rushed up to the entrance. "Hurry, everyone! Into the mountain!"

The four kids, with Max and Khan leading the way, charged between the raging fire monsters.

They ran into the opening.

They entered the world of the volcano.

Five

Smoke and Mirrors

They dashed through the dark entrance and found themselves in a vast cavern. The red glow from a lava pool lit the high walls around them.

"Phew! It smells burned in here," Neal whispered, creeping up behind Eric and Keeah. "Sort of like that brick oven pizza place back home."

"Without the good pizza smell," Eric added.

"Sparr is good at burning things," Khan said. "I hope to repay him for attacking my village."

Julie shivered. "You know, most people don't go inside a volcano. I hope we can get out."

"If we're careful, we will," Keeah said. "Now, first things first. Which way do we go?"

The cavern around them was dark and smoky. But it was empty. In the flickering red light, they saw a rough path dug out of the rock.

The path wound downward into the earth.

Eric knew where it led.

He wasn't sure *how* he knew, but he knew.

It led to the center of the volcano.

"We have to follow that path all the

way down," he said. "I have a feeling that's where Sparr keeps the Eye. Down there."

"How can you be sure?" Julie asked.

"Because the center is probably the scariest place anybody can think of," Keeah replied. "And Sparr would want to make it as hard as possible for anyone to find the Eye."

Max nodded. "And it *will* be harder, once he knows we are here."

Eric wondered how long it would take Sparr to find them poking around his secret hiding place. And what he would do when he did.

Khan sniffed. "Danger this way. Let's go on."

They all started down the winding path. It led below the level they had entered on, passing boiling pools that hissed and bubbled loudly.

They were being as quiet as they could be.

"The rock is getting hotter," Max said, crawling along the jagged walls of the path. "I wonder how we'll know when we reach the center."

"That's where they keep the lava," Neal said.

"Phew!" Julie sniffed. "What's that smell?"

Neal looked down. "My sneakers are on fire! Yikes! Now I know where my dream came from!" He stamped his sneakers until the fire went out. "Oh, man, that really hurt!"

"So do Ninns!" Eric hissed. "Quiet!"

The kids crept down to still another level.

The air was even hotter and smokier. It smelled worse. Keeah stopped. She held up her hand. "There's a cave up ahead," she whispered. "Something's moving. I saw a shadow —"

Suddenly, a figure stepped out of the cave.

"Guards, seize them!" a man said in a deep, snarly tone. The man was Lord Sparr!

"Whoa!" Neal gasped. "Let's get out of here!"

Everyone rushed back up the path, but Julie didn't move. She seemed frozen to the spot.

"Guards, seize them!" the sorcerer repeated in the same deep tone as before.

Eric dashed back to her. "Julie, come on! Sparr's the bad guy! Do I have to drag you out?"

"Wait a sec," Julie whispered.

"Wait?" Eric cried. "For big greasy Ninns to come clomping over and grab us? Come on!"

But Julie wouldn't budge. Seconds

passed and there were no clomping footsteps. No greasy Ninn claws grabbing them.

Instead, Sparr turned stiffly and walked back into the cave. He appeared to touch the cave wall, but didn't quite touch it.

"See¿" Julie murmured. "That's not him —"

"We'll be caught, you two!" Max cried, scampering up behind them with the others.

Julie laughed. "No, look. That isn't Sparr. I mean, it's not really Sparr. That is — I don't know what — special effects or something."

The figure strode forward again, not even blinking. Neal cringed as it stared icily at them.

"Guards, seize them!" Sparr repeated.

"Ha!" Julie said. "I don't think so, Sparr." Then she leaned forward and slapped the

sorcerer in the arm. Her hand went right through!

"Whoa!" Neal whispered.

"See what I mean?" Julie said.

Keeah nodded. "Maybe Sparr created a double to take his place because the jewel burned him. Maybe the real Sparr is hurt."

"Maybe it's done with mirrors," Eric said.

"Weird," said Neal, peering around the figure. "He's Sparr, but he's fake."

"Well, *they* aren't!" Max suddenly chirped.

The spider troll pointed at two giant red-faced Ninn soldiers. They came clomping down the passage right toward them.

"I thought I smelled something bad," Khan snorted, starting to run.

The Ninns grunted and hissed.

They pulled out big swords.

"GET THEM!" yelled the Ninns.

Six

Meeting the Witch

"Get the small ones!" the Ninns shouted. "And the purple Lumpy king, too!"

The kids shot down the passage like rockets.

They dived into the first cave they came to.

The two Ninns didn't see them. They charged away down the passage, thumping their big feet.

Eric breathed a sigh of relief. Then he

looked around. "Uh . . . who picked this cave?"

"You did!" Neal answered.

Instead of a hot, red cave, the space inside was tinted blue. A cool breeze blew through it.

And in the center was a large pool of the bluest water imaginable.

The surface of the water glistened and sparkled like glass.

"Whoa!" said Julie, peering around. "This is the place from my dream! This is what I saw!"

"Do you think it's regular water?" Eric asked.

"I don't see anything yucky," Neal said.

"I don't like it," Khan murmured.

Keeah stepped closer. "Let me test it out."

Keeah had told the kids she had powers. But they weren't exactly sure what she could do.

"Careful," said Eric. "This is Kano, don't forget. Sparr's home base."

Keeah reached for the water.

Suddenly, something with scaly skin slithered toward her from the far side of the pool.

"Watch out!" Julie cried. "A sea monster!"

Keeah jerked back from the edge of the pool.

A long, green, scaly tail broke the surface with a loud splash. It slapped down hard, and seconds later a head popped up out of the water.

It was the head of a woman!

"A mermaid!" Eric whispered.

Her skin was white, her lips were black. She had long, wet, green hair. Her shoul-

ders were dark and scaly. And her deep blue eyes narrowed as she looked from one child to the next.

"No," said Max. "Not a mermaid."

The woman spoke. "Who — are — you?"

Her voice was eerie and deep.

It seemed to come from every corner of the cave. Each word echoed off the stony walls.

Keeah glanced at her friends, then turned to the woman. "Uh . . . we . . . I am Keeah, Princess of Droon. And these are my friends."

The woman's eyes didn't move. "Friends from the Upper World. Sparr has spoken of you."

Julie shuddered. "What did he say about us? What does Lord Sparr know about us?"

But the woman didn't answer. She

turned to Keeah. "You have come for the Eye of Dawn."

Eric jumped. "How did you know that?"

"I am Demither," the woman said. "Some people say I am a witch. I know many things."

Her spiked tail flipped up suddenly. Water splashed on the cave walls and hissed.

"I've heard of you," Max twittered. "My master, Galen, has spoken of your evil deeds."

"Some choose to be evil," the witch said. "Some are forced to be evil." Demither clenched her teeth and dove under the water again.

"Something's weird," Eric said. "She looks like she's in pain or something."

"I am still afraid to trust her," Max said.

Splash! Demither rose again. "The Eye is in the Room of Fire!" She closed her eyes and groaned. "Cross the Bridge of Ice, and you will find it."

Keeah stepped to the edge. "If you know things, can you tell me how my mother died —"

"Your mother is alive!" the witch cried sharply. "Like me, she is cursed, in prison!"

Keeah gasped. "Prison! Here in the volcano?"

"Not here . . . everywhere!" the witch cried. "Find her. Help her — *as no one has helped me!*"

Seven

The Fierce Beast

The four kids all stared at Demither.

"So it's true!" Keeah exclaimed. "My mother is alive. I knew she was! I knew it!"

"Why are you helping us?" Eric asked the witch. "I thought you were a friend of Sparr."

"Friend!" the woman shrieked. She rose up ten feet in the air. Her scaly skin rippled and twisted as she curved up toward the cave's ceiling. "I — am — a — friend — of — no — one!"

"Wait," Keeah pleaded. "I need to know —"

But the witch's scaly body slithered back silently into the dark pool. The water hissed loudly as she passed under it.

Then the surface went still.

Demither was gone.

The kids looked at one another for a long time.

"It sounds like Sparr is forcing the witch to do bad stuff," Julie said finally. "Maybe he cursed your mother, Keeah."

"I don't like it," Max said. "Demither could be lying to us."

Keeah stared at the pool. "We need the Eye."

"Can the Eye do good things, too?" Eric asked her. "Can it, like, heal people and stuff?"

Keeah nodded. "Galen told me once that the jewel does what its owner wants it to."

"Cool," Neal mumbled. "I wish my dog did."

"But it is dangerous, too," said Khan. "Even Sparr was hurt by its power."

Eric turned to Keeah. "We'll get the Eye back for you. We'll do it, I promise. No matter —"

He never got a chance to finish.

Clomp, clomp! Heavy footsteps rushed toward the blue cave from the path outside.

"Hurry, or we'll be trapped!" Julie cried. She and Neal slipped out, with Max and Khan scrambling behind. But Eric and Keeah couldn't make it.

"Behind these rocks, quick!" Eric said to her.

They jumped behind a low pile of rocks near the cave entrance.

In marched ten Ninns. In between them crawled a strange, dark beast. It snarled and growled at the nervous-looking Ninns.

The beast stopped at the pool's edge.

"What is that thing?" Eric whispered to Keeah.

The princess shook her head. "I don't know."

The beast yowled sharply, as if it were hurt.

In the dim light, Eric could see that the creature had four thick, clawed legs and a long body.

Its skin was black and bumpy from its large head all the way to its long, spiked tail.

On the top of its head were rows of large, pointed ears, like bat's ears.

Eric's stomach turned just looking at the ugly thing. He swallowed hard. "It's some kind of weird, horrible monster."

"Is this Sparr's secret weapon?" Keeah asked.

Eric struggled to keep his food down. "Maybe *this* is his secret. The one in my dream. The secret Sparr thought I knew. He keeps a monster for a pet."

Suddenly, the creature charged forward and leaped to the pool. It began to slurp loudly.

"Let's get out of here," Keeah whispered. "That thing could turn on us."

Eric began to tremble. "Wait . . ."

They watched the beast drink and drink.

Eric turned to Keeah. She looked at him.

Then they looked back at the creature.

Their eyes went wide with amazement.

"No!" Eric gasped softly. "It . . . can't . . . be!"

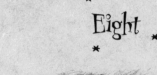

Eight

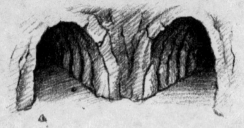

Sparr's Secret?

As the beast slurped from the pool, it began to change. Its dark, spiky hide shrank away. One by one, the sharp claws shriveled. Two became hands, two became feet.

Pale, smooth skin formed over the head.

The creature's arms and legs began to grow longer.

Suddenly, the thing stood upright. Like a man.

All that remained of the monster were two pointed fins growing behind the ears.

Eric caught his breath. "Holy crow!"

The man threw his powerful arms into the air.

Deep, frightening laughter filled the cavern.

The man was Lord Sparr!

Without taking a breath, Eric and Keeah crept from the cave and ran quickly down the path.

"I can't believe it!" Eric whispered. "Sparr's a monster! A creature! A creepy beast thing!"

Keeah shivered. "Remember what Khan told us? The Eye of Dawn burned Sparr. Maybe it did worse things. Maybe it made him like this."

"Yeah, and he drinks from the pool to make himself human again," Eric said. "Because if he doesn't, he changes back into this — *thing*! Maybe *that's* his secret! Just like in my dream!"

Julie, Neal, Max, and Khan ran up to them.

"Are you guys okay?" Julie asked.

"You'll never believe what we saw!" Keeah said. "There was a —"

But Keeah didn't get to finish.

Lord Sparr stepped out of the shadows.

"Ninns! I have found them!" the sorcerer said in a snarly tone. His eyes flashed at the kids.

Neal laughed suddenly. "Oh, look. Mr. Special Effects is back! Guys, let me handle this."

"Neal, no!" Eric began.

Neal stuck his hands behind his ears and wiggled them as if they were fins. "Fake Sparr! Fake Sparr!"

Then he marched up to the sorcerer, stood right in front of him, and made a fist. "Now, I'm going to punch right through your bogus self!"

"Neal, don't," Keeah said. "It's really —"

Smack! Neal's fist stopped at Sparr's arm.

Neal frowned. "It's supposed to go through." He turned to Julie. "It went through for you."

"Neal . . ." Julie said.

Neal punched Sparr again. *Smack!*

"Oh, now I get it." Neal said quietly. "Ouch."

"NINNS!" the sorcerer shouted at the top of his lungs. The passageway filled with red-faced warriors.

The kids were surrounded.

Keeah's eyes burned with anger. "We know your secret, Sparr. You're a monster!"

"A creepy one!" said Eric. "Much creepier than you are now. Which is pretty creepy!"

The sorcerer's lips curled into an evil snarl. His eyes darkened. His purple fins began to curl.

"Now you can never leave!" he said. His muscled hand clamped down on Neal's shoulder.

Neal screeched. "It's because I did hands behind the ears, isn't it? You didn't like that."

"You leave my best friend alone!" Eric yelled. He jumped as hard as he could on Sparr's feet.

"Ahhh!" The sorcerer released Neal.

"I sniff an escape this way!" Khan yelled.

The six friends shot away down the narrow passage. They were still going deeper into the volcano.

Sparr leaped into the air after them. He

flew like a bullet, swooping through the tunnels, screaming strange words. *"Selam! Ala! Kwitt!"*

"Same to you!" Julie shouted back.

Eric and Keeah were in the lead, threading through the curving passages.

Suddenly, the passage split before them. Two tunnels lay ahead. Both were dark.

"Left! Left!" Keeah cried.

Eric flashed a look at his hands. He couldn't decide. *Left? Left!* He kept running toward the passages. He ran faster.

"Hurry!" the princess shouted.

Right? Left! Huh? This is so dumb! With all the smoke and darkness, he couldn't even see!

Eric picked one dark passage, running into it as fast as he could. He wanted to get as far as possible from Sparr. He'd discovered his secret.

But now sounds were swirling all around him.

Hissing and bubbling. Clomping and stomping. Eric stole a quick look backward.

It was dark. He couldn't see Keeah anywhere.

He slowed to a stop. "Guys? Are you back there in the dark? Oh, man, please answer!"

No answer.

Eric swallowed hard. "Sp-Sparr? Please *don't* answer. . . ."

No answer. Eric was alone in the dark.

He couldn't tell front from back. Right from left. Up from down.

"Where am I?" he breathed.

Splurt — ssss! A sudden fiery splash of lava burst from the volcano floor. It flashed against the walls of a vast cavern. Smoking red lava bubbled and hissed away into the far distance.

"It's a lake," Eric gasped. "A lake of lava!"

He knew right away where he was.

He had found it.

The Room of Fire.

Nine

Fountain of Danger

Splursh! The fiery column spurted again. It was coming from a strange fountain on a small island in the center of the lake. The fountain was formed of craggy, hardened lava.

Then Eric noticed something else.

Near the top of the fountain, and sheltered from its spray, was a dome of glass.

Inside the dome was a strange black object.

An armored glove with a red jewel on it.

"The Eye of Dawn!" Eric said to himself. "Just like Demither said."

But the fountain lay in the center of a lake of burning, bubbling lava. He would burn to a crisp if he took one step into it. Then he remembered what else Demither had told them.

Cross the Bridge of Ice.

Eric circled the shore of the lava lake. Something about the lava's surface seemed strange.

Some parts of it didn't move the same as in other places. He bent down at one spot and gazed across the top of the lava.

A narrow strip of something clear lay just above the bubbling surface. It looked like a strip of glass, stretching from the shore to the island.

"The Bridge of Ice!" he said.

Carefully, he stepped onto the bridge. It

held him. He took another step. He felt as if he were walking a tightrope. But he kept going.

Soon he was halfway across. Halfway to the island. To the stone fountain itself. To the Eye!

Splursh! The fountain exploded with a giant spurt of molten rock. Fiery spray shot to the ceiling and showered back down to the giant lake.

Tssss! The rocks hit the surface all around him.

But Eric kept going. He couldn't turn back. Not until he got what they had come for.

"We have to stop Lord Sparr," he said firmly.

Splursh! The fountain went off again. *Tssss!*

Eric timed it to see how long he had until the next eruption. "One Mississippi, two Mississippi, three Mississippi, four Mississippi —"

Splursh! Tssss!

"Four seconds," Eric told himself. He took a deep breath, ran to the end of the bridge, and sprang off. He landed at the base of the fountain.

One Mississippi . . .

In two quick moves, he was up to the top of the fountain. Using a rock, he broke the glass dome and grabbed the black glove.

Two Mississippi . . .

He jumped down to the base of the fountain. But the rocks were covered with a thin layer of ashes. His sneakers slid on them. He tried to steady himself. He hit the ground. "Ooof!"

Three Mississippi . . .

Plonk! The glove fell from his hand.

"No!" Eric yelled out. He reached out

wildly for the glove. His fingers fumbled for it.

Four Mississippi!

SPLURSH! Molten rocks exploded up from the fountain to the ceiling. Then they began to fall.

Eric grabbed the glove and pulled it on.

The fiery rocks seemed to aim right for him.

"Nooooo!" he screamed, throwing his arms up to shield himself from the burning rocks.

Suddenly, the Eye of Dawn began to glow.

Blam! Blam! Blam! Flashes of red light shot from the glove's fingertips. The molten rocks blasted apart in midair. One after another, the chunks of molten stone exploded to nothing.

Eric's hand was going crazy. He couldn't

control the Eye. It blew up everything in sight.

Blam! Blam! The fountain itself shattered into a thousand pieces.

"Whoa!" Eric cried. "Glove, stop! Eye, stop!"

But the Red Eye of Dawn wouldn't stop.

Eric struggled to his feet and rushed onto the bridge of ice. Then the Eye forced his hand around and blasted the bridge! *Ka-whoom!*

He dived to shore as the bridge exploded into a million little pieces.

The walls of the cavern were starting to quake. The volcano floor was rumbling. The lava lake swelled. Waves churned and splashed.

"Uh-oh!" he gasped, scrambling up. "I think I started something! And it's not good!"

"Eric!" someone shouted.

He turned. It was Keeah, running into the cavern. Behind her were Julie, Neal, Khan, and Max.

"I've got the Eye!" Eric shouted to them. "But I can't control it too well!"

Blam! Blam! The glove blasted the black walls two feet away from his friends' heads.

"We get the idea!" Keeah shouted. She ran over and grabbed Eric's hand. Suddenly, the glove became steady. It seemed as if a power moved through Keeah's hand to his own.

"Good work, Eric!" Julie cried. "You did it!"

"Save the praise for later," Max chirped. "Here comes Lord Sparr!"

"Grab Eric's hand," shouted Keeah.

Neal, Julie, Max, and Khan put their hands over Keeah's and Eric's. Keeah focused the glove toward the far wall.

KA-WHOOM! The Eye blew a hole

clear through the volcano wall! Daylight shone through the hole.

The force of the Eye pulled the kids from the ground. It shot them through the rocky passage like a rocket.

"I will follow you — forever!" cried Lord Sparr, charging in as the black walls of his volcano home began to crumble.

Ten

The Door Home

"Whoaaa!" Eric shrieked as the six friends barreled out through the volcano at top speed.

Then — *splat-at-at-at-at-at!*

They hit a wall. Luckily, it was a soft wall. It was a wall made of sand. It was a sand dune.

"We're outside!" Julie yelled. "Yahoo!"

"There they are!" cried a voice. Galen rode up quickly. Behind him, the Lumpies had just finished tying the fire monsters in a giant knot.

"Yes!" Max chittered. "My master is safe!"

"We have the Eye!" Keeah called out.

Galen's eyes lit up. "My friends, you have done well!" Carefully, he took the glove from Eric. He closed his hands around it and put it safely in a golden box in Leep's saddlebag.

"We must leave Kano at once," the wizard said. "Keeah, your father's ship is waiting at the coast. The stairs to the Upper World have appeared there, too. Max, come. Hurry, everyone. Hurry!"

Max jumped up on Leep's head. "The way out is in the West! The old riddle says, it cannot be seen where it is!"

Eric sighed. "Another riddle? Can't anything in Droon be easy?"

"This will make it easier," Khan said. *Flump!* He tossed something heavy on the sand. "A carpet from Pasha."

"A flying carpet!" Julie exclaimed.

"The perfect escape vehicle!" Neal added.

"Better hurry," Khan cried, sniffing the smoky air. "Groggles — lots of them. Coming fast!"

Out of the smoke came dozens of Ninns on their ugly flying lizards called groggles. Huge flapping wings darkened the dark air even more.

Kaww! Kaww! the groggles cried.

"Let's see how fast this baby can go," Julie said. "Everybody on Pasha's rug! Now — *fly!*"

Whoosh! The carpet lifted into the wind and soared up over the volcano. As Galen, Max, Khan, and the Lumpies galloped away, Julie tugged at a corner, and the carpet shot out across the dunes.

But the flying groggles were fast, too. They chased the kids for mile after mile, getting closer and closer.

Eric scanned the desert ahead. In the middle of the dunes was a single rock. It was tall and wide and stuck straight up from the desert floor.

"Watch out for that rock," Keeah said.

"Yeah," Neal added, "we definitely don't want to crash into that!"

"Right . . ." Eric began. Then he shook his head. "No, head *for* it! The riddle says that the way out cannot be seen where it is. The way out is *through the rock*!"

"Are you sure?" Julie asked.

"Trust me!" Eric said.

Kaww! The groggles were right behind them.

The rock was right ahead of them.

"It sure looks solid!" Neal cried, shutting his eyes and clutching the carpet tight. "I hope this works!"

Around the rock was open air, stretching into the distance. Still, the kids dove for the rock.

They went . . . *into* the rock.

Whoosh! At the moment the carpet hit the rock, the rock became an opening. At the same moment, the air around it became solid rock.

"Agh!" the Ninns cried. Their groggles lurched away, nearly smashing into the wall of rock.

"Hooray!" Eric held on tight as they swept into a world of trees and rivers and meadows.

The air was clear and fresh. It smelled sweet.

"We're out of Kano!" Keeah said, pointing to the distance. "And heading for the coast."

Minutes later, they landed on a sandy shore. A blue ocean rolled gently to the distant horizon.

And the stairs back to Eric's house glittered nearby, hovering inches above the beach.

A grand wooden ship was floating in a peaceful bay. It had white-and-pink sails and a blue smokestack. The ship's sides swept back from a sharp point in front to twin wings in the rear.

"Today, we won," Keeah said. "We learned that Sparr is some kind of — creature."

"He turns back into it sometimes," Eric said. "And he needs to drink from the witch's pool."

"It's weird," said Neal. "How all our dreams sort of came true. . . ."

Eric shook his head. "I guess there are still lots of secrets about Droon we don't know."

"Like the whole story about the witch, Demither," Julie added. "She was strange. Kind of sad, too."

Keeah breathed in, smiling. "She said my mother is alive, under a curse somewhere. If she is, I'm going to find her and set her free."

"We'll help you," Eric said. "We'll be back as soon as we can."

"Definitely," Neal said. "Count me in!"

"Count us all in," Julie added.

As the kids made their way to the magic stairs, a pilka whinnied behind them. *Hrrr!*

They turned to see Galen, Max, and Khan riding down the beach toward them. They waved.

"You're safe now," Eric said to Keeah. "I guess we'd better go before the stairs fade."

"The magic of Droon goes with you," Keeah said, waving. "It will tell you when to return!"

The three friends raced up the magic stairs. At the top, Eric turned to look back at Droon.

"I hope the adventure never ends," Julie said.

Eric smiled. "Something tells me it never will. There are too many secrets we don't know yet."

"And too much work for us to do," Neal said.

Julie laughed. "There's plenty of work for us up here, too. In our normal lives. We said we'd clean up the basement, remember?"

They all stepped up into the room at the top of the stairs. Neal flicked the light switch.

Click! The land of Droon vanished. In its place was the plain old cement floor.

"We're home," Eric murmured. He put his hand on the doorknob and opened the door.

The three friends went out into the basement.

The messy, messy basement.

They got to work.

ABOUT THE AUTHOR

Tony Abbott is the author of more than two dozen funny novels for young readers, including the popular *Danger Guys* books and *The Weird Zone* series. Since childhood he has been drawn to stories that challenge the imagination, and, like Eric, Julie, and Neal, he often dreamed of finding doors that open to other worlds. Now that he is older — though not quite as old as Galen Longbeard — he believes he may have found some of those doors. They are called books. Tony Abbott was born in Ohio and now lives with his wife and two daughters in Connecticut.

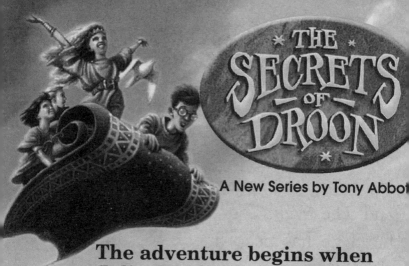